EL OMBÚ
SOUTH AMERICAN ROMANCES

W.H. HUDSON

British Library Cataloguing-in-Publication Data
A catalogue record for this book is available from the
British Library

William Henry Hudson

William Henry Hudson was born on 4 August 1841 in a borough of Quilmes (now Florecio Varela) in Greater Buenos Aires, Argentina. His parents, Daniel and Catherine Hudson, were American settlers of English and Irish origin. His father was a sheep farmer on a small farm in Argentina, but was sadly unsuccessful. He then turned to potato growing for a paltry existence and this led the family to near financial ruin.

Hudson spent his childhood exploring the local flora and fauna and observing the natural and human drama, on what was a lawless frontier at that time. At around fourteen or fifteen, Hudson became seriously ill with a bout of typhus, soon followed by rheumatic fever. These illnesses permanently affected his health and caused him to become more studious and contemplative. His parents obtained many books for him and his siblings to read and he occasionally had some formal education from a visiting school teacher. Charles Darwin's (1809-1882) *The Origin of Species* (1859), in particular, made a lasting impression on him.

Little is known about Hudson in the period following his parents' death. He became a wanderer, occasionally publishing his ornithological work in the *Proceedings of the Zoological Society*. He initially wrote in an English that was interlaced with Spanish idioms. He appears to have particularly loved Patagonia. Hudson immigrated to London, England in 1869, where he eventually became a British subject in 1900. In 1876 he married a much older woman and they lived precariously on the money earned from two boarding houses that she owned. She eventually inherited a house in Bayswater, London and the couple moved there.

Hudson produced a series of ornithological studies throughout his life, including *Argentine Ornithology* (1888-1899) and *British Birds* (1895). These books on ornithological studies attracted the attention of the statesman, Sir Edward Grey (1862-1933), who got Hudson a state pension in 1901. Hudson later achieved fame with his books on the English countryside, such as *Hampshire Day* (1903), *Afoot in England* (1909), and *A Shepherd's Life* (1910), which helped foster the back to nature movement of the 1920s and 1930s. His most famous fictional novel was *Green Mansions* (1904) which was an exotic romance about a traveller in the Guyana Jungle in Venezuela and his encounter with a mysterious forest girl who is half human and half bird. This romance and some of Hudson's other romances attracted the friendship of other fiction writers, such as Joseph Conrad (1857-

1924), Ford Madox Ford (1873-1939) and George Gissing (1857-1903). Hudson's most popular non-fiction novel was *Far Away and Long Ago* (1918) which recalls his childhood in Argentina. Some of his other titles include *Birds and Man* (1901), *A Little Lost Boy* (1905), *Tales of the Pampas* (1916), *Ralph Herne* (1923), and *Mary's Little Lamb* (1929).

Away from his literary work, Hudson was a founding member of the Royal Society for the Protection of Birds. Towards the end of his life he moved to Worthing, Sussex, England. He died on 18 August 1922 and is buried at Broadwater and Worthing Cemetery in Worthing where his epitaph refers to his love of birds and green places. Even after his death, Hudson had a huge legacy. In Argentina where he is known as Guillermo Enrique Hudson, his work is considered to belong to the national literature. Ernest Hemingway (1899-1961) also famously refers to Hudson's early book *The Purple Land* (1885) in his novel *The Sun Also Rises* (1926) and again to Hudson's *Far Away and Long Ago* in his posthumous novel, *The Garden of Eden* (1986). Hudson has also had two South American bird species named after him as well as a town in Berazategui Partidd and several other public places and institutions.

CONTENTS

EL OMBÚ

This history of a house that had been was told in the shade, one summer's day, by Nicandro, that old man to whom we all loved to listen, since he could remember and properly narrate the life of every person he had known in his native place, near to the lake of Chascomus, on the southern pampas of Buenos Ayres.

CHAPTER I

IN all this district, though you should go twenty leagues to this way and that, you will not find a tree as big as this ombú, standing solitary, where there is no house; therefore it is known to all as " the ombú," as if but one existed; and the name of all this estate, which is now ownerless and ruined, is El Ombú. From one of the higher branches, if you can climb, you will see the lake of Chascomus, two thirds of a league away, from shore to shore, and the village on its banks. Even smaller things will you see on a clear day; perhaps a red line moving across the water—a flock of flamingos flying in their usual way. A great tree standing alone, with no house near it; only the old brick foundations of a house, so overgrown with grass and weeds that you have to look closely to find them. When I am out with my flock in the summer time, I often come here to sit in the shade. It is near the main road; travellers, droves of cattle, the diligence, and bullock-carts pass in sight. Sometimes, at noon, I find a traveller

1

resting in the shade, and if he is not sleeping we talk and he tells me the news of that great world my eyes have never seen. They say that sorrow and at last ruin comes upon the house on whose roof the shadow of the ombú tree falls; and on that house which now is not, the shadow of this tree came every summer day when the sun was low. They say, too, that those who sit much in the ombú shade become crazed. Perhaps, sir, the bone of my skull is thicker than in most men, since I have been accustomed to sit here all my life, and though now an old man I have not yet lost my reason. It is true that evil fortune came to the old house in the end; but into every door sorrow must enter—sorrow and death that comes to all men; and every house must fall at last.

Do you hear the mangangá, the carpenter bee, in the foliage over our heads? Look at him, like a ball of shining gold among the green leaves, suspended in one place, humming loudly! Ah, señor, the years that are gone, the people that have lived and died, speak to me thus audibly when I am sitting here by myself. These are memories; but there are other things that come back to us from the past; I mean ghosts. Sometimes, at midnight, the whole tree, from its great roots to its topmost leaves, is seen from a distance shining like white fire. What is that fire, seen of so many, which does not scorch the leaves? And, sometimes, when a traveller lies down here to sleep the siesta, he hears sounds of footsteps coming and going, and noises of dogs and fowls, and of children shouting and laughing, and voices of people talking; but when he starts up and listens, the sounds grow faint, and seem at last to pass away into the tree with a low murmur as of wind among the leaves.

As a small boy, from the time when I was able, at the age of about six years, to climb on to a pony and ride, I knew this tree. It was then what it is now ; five men with their arms stretched to their utmost length could hardly encircle it. And the house stood there, where you see a bed of nettles—a long, low house, built of bricks, when there were few brick houses in this district, with a thatched roof.

The last owner was just touching on old age. Not that he looked aged ; on the contrary, he looked what he was, a man among men, a head taller than most, with the strength of an ox ; but the wind had blown a little sprinkling of white ashes into his great beard and his hair, which grew to his shoulders like the mane of a black horse. That was Don Santos Ugarte, known to all men in this district as the White Horse, on account of the whiteness of his skin where most men look dark ; also because of that proud temper and air of authority which he had. And for still another reason—the number of children in this neighbourhood of which he was said to be the father. In all houses, for many leagues around, the children were taught to reverence him, calling him " uncle," and when he appeared they would run and, dropping on their knees before him, cry out " *Bendicion mi tio*." He would give them his blessing ; then, after tweaking a nose and pinching an ear or two, he would flourish his whip over their heads to signify that he had done with them, and that they must quickly get out of his way.

3

EL OMBÚ

These were children of the wind, as the saying is, and the desire of his heart was for a legitimate son, an Ugarte by name, who would come after him at El Ombú, as he had come after his father. But though he had married thrice, there was no son born, and no child. Some thought it a mystery that one with so many sons should yet be without a son. The mystery, friend, was only for those who fail to remember that such things are not determined by ourselves. We often say, that He who is above us is too great to concern Himself with our small affairs. There are so many of us ; and how shall He, seated on his throne at so great a distance, know all that passes in his dominions ! But Santos was no ordinary person, and He who was greater than Santos had doubtless had his attention drawn to this man ; and had considered the matter, and had said, "You shall not have your desire; for though you are a devout man, one who gives freely of his goods to the church and my poor, I am not wholly satisfied with you." And so it came to pass that he had no son and heir.

His first two wives had died, so it was said, because of his bitterness against them. I only knew the third—Doña Mericie, a silent, sad woman, who was of less account than any servant, or any slave in the house. And I, a simple boy, what could I know of the secrets of her heart ? Nothing ! I only saw her pale and silent and miserable, and because her eyes followed me, I feared her, and tried always to keep out of her way. But one morning, when I came to El Ombú and went into the kitchen, I found her there alone, and before I could escape she caught me in

4

her arms, and lifting me off my feet strained me against her breast, crying, *hijo de mi alma*, and I knew not what beside ; and calling God's blessing on me, she covered my face with kisses. Then all at once, hearing Santos' voice without, she dropped me and remained like a woman of stone, staring at the door with scared eyes.

She, too, died in a little while, and her disappearance made no difference in the house, and if Santos wore a black band on his arm, it was because custom demanded it and not because he mourned for her in his heart.

CHAPTER II

THAT silent ghost of a woman being gone, no one could say of him that he was hard; nor could anything be said against him except that he was not a saint, in spite of his name. But, sir, we do not look for saints among strong men, who live in the saddle, and are at the head of big establishments. If there was one who was a father to the poor it was Santos; therefore he was loved by many, and only those who had done him an injury or had crossed him in any way had reason to fear and hate him. But let me now relate what I, a boy of ten, witnessed one day in the year 1808. This will show you what the man's temper was; and his courage, and the strength of his wrists.

It was his custom to pay a visit every two or three months to a monastery at a distance of half-a-day's journey from El Ombú.

He was greatly esteemed by the friars, and whenever he went to see them he had a led horse to carry his presents to the Brothers;—a side of fat beef, a sucking-pig or two, a couple of lambs, when they were in season, a few fat turkeys and ducks, a bunch of big partridges, a brace or two of armadillos, the breast and wings of a fat ostrich; and in summer, a dozen ostriches' eggs, and I know not what besides.

EL OMBÚ

One evening I was at El Ombú, and was just starting for home, when Santos saw me, and cried out, " Get off and let your horse go, Nicandro. I am going to the monastery to-morrow, and you shall ride the laden horse, and save me the trouble of leading it. You will be like a little bird perched on his back and he will not feel your few ounces' weight. You can sleep on a sheepskin in the kitchen, and get up an hour before daybreak."

The stars were still shining when we set out on our journey the next morning, in the month of June, and when we crossed the river Sanboronbón at sunrise the earth was all white with hoar frost. At noon, we arrived at our destination, and were received by the friars, who embraced and kissed Santos on both cheeks, and took charge of our horses. After breakfast in the kitchen, the day being now warm and pleasant, we went and sat out of doors to sip maté and smoke, and for an hour or longer, the conversation between Santos and the Brothers had been going on when, all at once, a youth appeared coming at a fast gallop towards the gate, shouting as he came, " Los Ingleses ! Los Ingleses ! " We all jumped up and ran to the gate, and climbing up by the posts and bars, saw at a distance of less than half-a-league to the east, a great army of men marching in the direction of Buenos Ayres. We could see that the foremost part of the army had come to a halt on the banks of a stream which flows past the monastery and empties itself into the Plata, two leagues farther east. The army was all composed of infantry, but a great many persons on horseback could be seen following it. and these,

7

the young man said, were neighbours who had come out to look at the English invaders ; and he also said that the soldiers, on arriving at the stream, had begun to throw away their blankets, and that the people were picking them up. Santos hearing this, said he would go and join the crowd, and mounting his horse and followed by me, and by two of the Brothers, who said they wished to get a few blankets for the monastery, we set out at a gallop for the stream.

Arrived at the spot, we found that the English, not satisfied with the ford, which had a very muddy bottom, had made a new crossing-place for themselves by cutting down the bank on both sides, and that numbers of blankets had been folded and laid in the bed of the stream where it was about twenty-five yards wide. Hundreds of blankets were also being thrown away, and the people were picking them up and loading their horses with them. Santos at once threw himself into the crowd and gathered about a dozen blankets, the best he could find, for the friars ; then he gathered a few for himself and ordered me to fasten them on the back of my horse.

The soldiers, seeing us scrambling for the blankets, were much amused ; but when one man among us cried out, " These people must be mad to throw their blankets away in cold weather—perhaps their red jackets will keep them warm when they lie down to-night "—there was one soldier who understood, and could speak Spanish, and he replied, " No, sirs, we have no further need of blankets. When we next sleep it will be in the best beds in the capitol." Then Santos shouted back, " That, sirs, will perhaps be a sleep from which some of you will never awake." That speech attracted their attention to Santos, and the soldier who had spoken before returned, " There are not many men like you in these parts, therefore what you say does not alarm us." Then they looked at the friars fastening the blankets Santos had given them on to their horses, and seeing that they wore heavy iron spurs strapped on their bare feet, they shouted with laughter, and the one who talked with us cried out, " We are sorry, good Brothers, that we have not boots as well as blankets to give you."

But our business was now done, and bidding good-bye to the friars, we set out on our return journey, Santos saying that we should be at home before midnight.

It was past the middle of the afternoon, we having ridden about six leagues, when we spied at a distance ahead a great number of mounted men scattered about over the plain, some standing still, others galloping this way or that.

" El pato ! el pato ! " cried Santos with excitement, " Come, boy, let us go and watch the battle while it is near, and when it is passed on we will go our way. Urging his horse to a gallop, I following, we came to where the men were struggling for the ball, and stood for a while looking on. But it was not in him to remain a mere spectator for long ; never did he see a cattlemarking, or parting, or races, or a dance, or any game, and above all games el Pato, but he must have a part in it. Very soon he dismounted to throw off some of the heaviest parts of his horse-gear, and ordering me to take them up on my horse and follow him, he rode in among the players.

EL OMBÚ

About forty or fifty men had gathered at that spot, and were sitting quietly on their horses in a wide circle, waiting to see the result of a struggle for the Pato between three men who had hold of the ball. They were strong men, well mounted, each resolved to carry off the prize from the others. Sir, when I think of that sight, and remember that the game is no longer played because of the Tyrant who forbade it, I am ready to cry out that there are no longer men on these plains where I first saw the light! How they tugged and strained and sweated, almost dragging each other out of the saddle, their trained horses leaning away, digging their hoofs into the turf, as when they resist the shock of a lassoed animal, when the lasso stiffens and the pull comes! One of the men was a big, powerful mulatto, and the bystanders, thinking the victory would be his, were only waiting to see him wrest the ball from the others to rush upon and try to deprive him of it before he could escape from the crowd.

Santos refused to stand inactive, for was there not a fourth handle to the ball to be grasped by another fighter? Spurring his horse into the group, he very soon succeeded in getting hold of the disengaged handle. A cry of resentment at this action on the part of a stranger went up from some of those who were looking on, mixed with applause at the daring from others, while the three men who had been fighting against each other, each one for himself, now perceived that they had a common enemy. Excited as they were by the struggle, they could not but be startled at the stranger's appearance—that huge man on a big horse, so white-skinned and long-haired, with a

10

black beard, that came down over his breast, and who showed them, when he threw back his poncho, the knife that was like a sword and the big brass-barrelled pistol worn at his waist. Very soon after he joined in the fray all four men came to the earth. But they did not fall together, and the last to go down was Santos, who would not be dragged off his horse, and in the end horse and man came down on the top of the others. In coming down, two of the men had lost their hold of the ball; last of all, the big mulatto, to save himself from being crushed under the falling horse, was forced to let go, and in his rage at being beaten, he whipped out his long knife against the stranger. Santos, too quick for him, dealt him a blow on the forehead with the heavy silver handle of his whip, dropping him stunned to the ground. Of the four, Santos alone had so far escaped injury, and rising and remounting, the ball still in his hand, he rode out from among them, the crowd opening on each side to make room for him.

Now in the crowd there was one tall, imposing-looking man, wearing a white poncho, many silver ornaments, and a long knife in an embossed silver sheath ; his horse, too, which was white as milk, was covered with silver trappings. This man alone raised his voice ; " Friends and comrades," he cried, " is this to be the finish ? If this stranger is permitted to carry the Pato away, it will not be because of his stronger wrist and better horse, but because he carries firearms. Comrades, what do you say ? "

But there was no answer. They had seen the power

and resolution of the man, and though they were many they preferred to let him go in peace. Then the man on a white horse, with a scowl of anger and contempt, turned from them and began following us at a distance of about fifty yards. Whenever Santos turned back to come to close quarters with him, he retired, only to turn and follow us again as soon as Santos resumed his course. In this way we rode till sunset. Santos was grave, but calm ; I, being so young, was in constant terror. " Oh, uncle," I whispered, " for the love of God fire your pistol at this man and kill him, so that he may not kill us ! "

Santos laughed. " Fool of a boy," he replied, " do you know that he wants me to fire at him ! He knows that I could not hit him at this distance, and that after discharging my pistol we should be equal, man to man, and knife to knife ; and who knows then which would kill the other ? God knows best, since He knows everything, and He has put it into my heart not to fire."

When it grew dark we rode slower, and the man then lessened the distance between us. We could hear the chink-chink of his silver trappings, and when I looked back I could see a white misty form following us like a ghost. Then, all at once, there came a noise of hoofs and a whistling sound of something thrown, and Santos' horse plunged and reared and kicked, then stood still trembling with terror. His hind legs were entangled in the bolas which had been thrown. With a curse Santos threw himself off, and, drawing his knife, cut the thong which bound the animal's legs, and remounting we went on as before, the white figure still following us.

12

EL OMBÚ

At length, about midnight, the Sanborombón was reached, at the ford where we had crossed in the morning, where it was about forty yards wide, and the water only high as the surcingle in the deepest parts.

" Let your heart be glad, Nicandro ! " said Santos, as we went down into the water ; " for our time is come now, and be careful to do as I bid you."

We crossed slowly, and coming out on the south side, Santos quietly dropped off his horse, and, speaking in a low voice, ordered me to ride slowly on with the two horses and wait for him in the road. He said that the man who followed would not see him crouching under the bank, and thinking it safe would cross over, only to receive the charge fired at a few yards distance.

That was an anxious interval that followed, I waiting alone, scarcely daring to breathe, staring into the darkness in fear of that white figure that was like a ghost, listening for the pistol shot. My prayer to heaven was to direct the bullet in its course, so that it might go to that terrible man's heart, and we be delivered from him. But there was no shot, and no sound except a faint chink of silver and sound of hoof-beats that came to my ears after a time, and soon ceased to be heard. The man, perhaps, had some suspicion of the other's plan and had given up the chase and gone away.

Nothing more do I remember of that journey which ended at El Ombú at cock-crow, except that at one spot Santos fastened a thong round my waist and bound me before and behind to the saddle to prevent my falling from my horse every time I went to sleep.

CHAPTER III

REMEMBER, Señor, that I have spoken of things that passed when I was small. The memories of that time are few and scattered, like the fragments of tiles and bricks and rusty iron which one may find half-buried among the weeds, where the house once stood. Fragments that once formed part of the building. Certain events, some faces, and some voices, I remember, but I cannot say the year. Nor can I say how many years had gone by after Doña Mericie's death, and after my journey to the monastery. Perhaps they were few, perhaps many. Invasions had come, wars with a foreigner and with the savages, and Independence, and many things had happened at a distance. He, Santos Ugarte, was older, I know, greyer, when that great misfortune and calamity came to one whom God had created so strong, so brave, so noble. And all on account of a slave, a youth born at El Ombú, who had been preferred above the others by his master. For, as it is said, we breed crows to pick our eyes out. But I will say nothing against that poor youth, who was the cause of the disaster, for it was not wholly his fault. Part of the fault was in Santos—his indomitable temper and his violence. And perhaps, too, the time was come when He who rules over all men had said, '' You have raised your voice and have ridden over others

14

long enough. Look, Santos! I shall set My foot upon you, and you shall be like a wild pumpkin at the end of summer, when it is dryer and more brittle that an empty egg-shell."

Remember that there were slaves in those days, also that there was a law fixing every man's price, old or young, so that if any slave went, money in hand, to his master and offered him the price of his liberty, from that moment he became a free man. It mattered not that his master wished not to sell him. So just was the law.

Of his slaves Santos was accustomed to say, " These are my children, and serve because they love me, not because they are slaves ; and if I were to offer his freedom to any one among them, he would refuse to take it." He saw their faces, not their hearts.

His favourite was Meliton, black but well favoured, and though but a youth, he had authority over the others, and dressed well, and rode his master's best horses, and had horses of his own. But it was never said of him that he gained that eminence by means of flattery and a tongue cunning to frame lies. On the contrary, he was loved by all, even by those he was set above, because of his goodness of heart and a sweet and gay disposition. He was one of those who can do almost anything better than others ; whatever his master wanted done, whether it was to ride a race, or break a horse, or throw a lasso, or make a bridle, or whip, or surcingle, or play on a guitar, or sing, or dance, it was Meliton, Meliton. There was no one like him.

EL OMBÚ

Now this youth cherished a secret ambition in his heart, and saved, and saved his money ; and at length one day he came with a handful of silver and gold to Santos, and said, " Master, here is the price of my freedom, take it and count it, and see that it is right, and let me remain at El Ombú to serve you henceforth without payment. But I shall no longer be a slave."

Santos took the money into his hand, and spoke, " It was for this then that you saved, even the money I gave you to spend and to run with, and the money you made by selling the animals I gave you—you saved it for this ! Ingrate, with a heart blacker than your skin ! Take back the money, and go from my presence, and never cross my path again if you wish for a long life." And with that he hurled the handful of silver and gold into the young man's face with such force that he was cut and bruised with the coins and well nigh stunned. He went back staggering to his horse, and mounting, rode away, sobbing like a child, the blood running from his face.

He soon left this neighbourhood and went to live at Las Vivoras, on the Vecino river, south of Dolores, and there made good use of his freedom, buying fat animals for the market ; and for a space of two years he prospered, and every man, rich or poor, was his friend. Nevertheless he was not happy, for his heart was loyal and he loved his old master, who had been a father to him, and desired above all things to be forgiven. And, at length, hoping that Santos had outlived his resentment and would be pleased to see him again, he one day came to El Ombú and asked to see the master.

16

The old man came out of the house and greeted him jovially. "Ha, Meliton," he cried with a laugh, "you have returned in spite of my warning. Come down from your horse and let me take your hand once more."

The other, glad to think he was forgiven, alighted, and advancing, put out his hand. Santos took it in his, only to crush it with so powerful a grip, that the young man cried out aloud, and blinded with tears of pain, he did not see that his master had the big brass pistol in his left hand, and did not know that his last moment had come. He fell with a bullet in his heart.

Look, señor, where I am pointing, twenty yards or so from the edge of the shadow of the ombú, do you see a dark green weed with a yellow flower on a tall stem growing on the short, dry grass? It was just there, on the very spot where the yellow flower is, that poor Meliton fell, and was left lying, covered with blood, until noon the next day. For no person dared take up the corpse until the Alcalde had been informed of the matter and had come to inquire into it.

Santos had mounted his horse and gone away without a word, taking the road to Buenos Ayres. He had done that for which he would have to pay dearly; for a life is a life, whether the skin be black or white, and no man can slay another deliberately, in cold blood, and escape the penalty. The law is no respecter of persons, and when he, who commits such a deed, is a man of substance, he must expect that Advocates and Judges, with all those who take up his cause, will bleed him well before they procure him a pardon.

EL OMBÚ

Ugarte cared nothing for that, he had been as good as his word, and the devil in his heart was satisfied. Only he would not wait at his estancia to be taken, nor would he go and give himself up to the authorities, who would then have to place him in confinement, and it would be many months before his liberation. That would be like suffocation to him ; to such a man a prison is like a tomb. No, he would go to Buenos Ayres and embark for Montevideo, and from that place he would put the matter in motion, and wait there until it was all settled and he was free to return to El Ombú.

Dead Meliton was taken away and buried in consecrated ground at Chascomus. Rain fell, and washed away the red stains on the ground. In the spring, the swallows returned and built their nests under the eaves ; but Ugarte came not back, nor did any certain tidings of him reach us. It was said, I know not whether truly or not, that the Advocate who defended him, and the Judge of First Instance, who had the case before him, had quarrelled about the division of the reward, and both being rich, proud persons, they had allowed themselves to forget the old man waiting there month after month for his pardon, which never came to him.

Better for him if he never heard of the ruin which had fallen on El Ombú during his long exile. There was no one in authority : the slaves, left to themselves, went away, and there was no person to restrain them. As for the cattle and horses, they were blown away like thistledown, and everyone was free to pasture his herds and flocks on the land.

EL OMBÚ

The house for a time was in charge of some person placed there by the authorities, but little by little it was emptied of its contents ; and at last it was abandoned, and for a long time no one could be found to live in it on account of the ghosts.

CHAPTER IV

THERE was living at that time, a few leagues from El Ombú, one Valerio de la Cueva, a poor man, whose all consisted of a small flock of three or four hundred sheep and a few horses. He had been allowed to make a small rancho, a mere hut, to shelter himself and his wife Donata and their one child, a boy named Bruno ; and to pay for the grass his few sheep consumed he assisted in the work at the estancia house. This poor man, hearing of El Ombú, where he could have house and ground for nothing, offered himself as occupant, and in time came with wife and child and his small flock, and all the furniture he possessed—a bed, two or three chairs, a pot and kettle, and perhaps a few other things. Such poverty El Ombú had not known, but all others had feared to inhabit such a place on account of its evil name, so that it was left for Valerio, who was a stranger in the district.

Tell me, señor, have you ever in your life met with a man, who was perhaps poor, or even clothed in rags, and who yet when you had looked at and conversed with him, has caused you to say : Here is one who is like no other man in the world ? Perhaps on rising and going out, on some clear morning in summer, he looked at the sun when it rose, and perceived an angel sitting in it, and as he gazed, something from that being fell upon and passed into and

20

remained with him. Such a man was Valerio. I have known no other like him.

" Come, friend Nicandro," he would say, " let us sit down in the shade and smoke our cigarettes, and talk of our animals. Here are no politics under this old ombú, no ambitions and intrigues and animosities—no bitterness except in these green leaves. They are our laurels— the leaves of the ombú. Happy Nicandro, who never knew the life of cities ! I wish that I, too, had seen the light on these quiet plains, under a thatched roof. Once I wore fine clothes and gold ornaments, and lived in a great house where there were many servants to wait on me. But happy I have never been. Every flower I plucked changed into a nettle to sting my hand. Perhaps that maleficent one, who has pursued me all my days, seeing me now so humbled and one with the poor, has left me and gone away. Yes, I am poor, and this frayed garment that covers me will I press to my lips because it does not shine with silk and gold embroidery. And this poverty which I have found will I cherish, and bequeath it as a precious thing to my child when I die. For with it is peace."

The peace did not last long ; for when misfortune has singled out a man for its prey, it will follow him to the end, and he shall not escape from it though he mount up to the clouds like the falcon, or thrust himself deep down into the earth like the armadillo.

Valerio had been two years at El Ombú when there came an Indian invasion on the southern frontier. There was no force to oppose it ; the two hundred men stationed

Y

21

at the Guardia del Azul had been besieged by a part of the invaders in the fort, while the larger number of the savages were sweeping away the cattle and horses from the country all round. An urgent order came to the commander at Chascomus to send a contingent of forty men from the department ; and I, then a young man of twenty, who had seen no service, was cited to appear at the Commandancia, in readiness to march. There I found that Valerio had also been cited, and from that moment we were together. Two days later we were at the Azul, the Indians having retired with their booty ; and when all the contingents from the various departments had come in, the commander, one Colonel Barboza, set out with about six hundred men in pursuit.

It was known that in their retreat the Indians had broken up their force into several parties, and that these had taken different directions, and it was thought that these bodies would reunite after a time, and that the larger number would return to their territory by way of Trinqué Lauquén, about seventy-five leagues west of Azul. Our Colonel's plan was to go quickly to this point and wait the arrival of the Indians. It was impossible that they, burdened with the thousands of cattle they had collected, could move fast, while we were burdened with nothing, the only animals we drove before us being our horses. These numbered about five thousand, but many were unbroken mares, to be used as food. Nothing but mare's flesh did we have to eat.

It was the depth of winter, and worse weather I have never known. In this desert I first beheld that whiteness

called snow, when the rain flies like cotton-down before
the wind, filling the air and whitening the whole earth.
All day and every day our clothes were wet, and there was
no shelter from the wind and rain at night, nor could we
make fires with the soaked grass and reeds, and wood
there was none, so that we were compelled to eat our
mare's flesh uncooked.

Three weeks were passed in this misery, waiting for the
Indians and seeking for them, with the hills of Gaumini
now before us in the south, and now on our left hand ;
and still no sight and no sign of the enemy. It seemed
as if the earth had opened and swallowed him up. Our
Colonel was in despair, and we now began to hope that he
would lead us back to the Azul.

In these circumstances one of the men, who was thinly
clad and had been suffering from a cough, dropped from
his horse, and it was then seen that he was likely to die,
and that in any case he would have to be left behind.
Finding that there was no hope for him, he begged that
those who were with him would remember, when they
were at home again, that he had perished in the desert and
that his soul was suffering in purgatory, and that they would
give something to the priests to procure him ease. When
asked by his officer to say who his relations were and where
they lived, he replied that he had no one belonging to him.
He said that he had spent many years in captivity among
the Indians at the Salinas Grandes, and that on his return
he had failed to find any one of his relations living in the
district where he had been born. In answer to further
questions, he said that he had been carried away when a

small boy, that the Indians on that occasion had invaded the Christian country in the depth of winter, and on their retreat, instead of returning to their own homes, they had gone east, towards the sea coast, and had encamped on a plain by a small stream called Curumamuel, at Los Tres Arroyos, where there was firewood and sweet water, and good grass for the cattle, and where they found many Indians, mostly women and children, who had gone thither to await their coming ; and at that spot they had remained until the spring.

The poor man died that night, and we gathered stones and piled them on his body so that the foxes and caranchos should not devour him.

At break of day next morning we were on horseback marching at a gallop toward sunrise, for our Colonel had determined to look for the Indians at that distant spot near the sea where they had hidden themselves from their pursuers so many years before. The distance was about seventy leagues, and the journey took us about nine days. And at last, in a deep valley near the sea, the enemy was discovered by our scouts, and we marched by night until we were within less than a league of their encampment, and could see their fires. We rested there for four hours, eating raw flesh and sleeping. Then every man was ordered to mount his best horse, and we were disposed in a half-moon, so that the free horses could easily be driven before us. The Colonel, sitting on his horse, addressed us. " Boys," he said, " you have suffered much, but now the victory is in our hands, and you shall not lose the reward. All the captives you take, and all the thousands

of horses and cattle we succeed in recovering, shall be sold
by public auction on our return, and the proceeds divided
among you."
He then gave the order, and we moved quietly on for a
space of half a league, and coming to the edge of the
valley saw it all black with cattle before us, and the
Indians sleeping in their camp ; and just when the sun
rose from the sea and God's light came over the earth,
with a great shout we charged upon them. In a moment
the multitude of cattle, struck with panic, began rushing
away, bellowing, in all directions, shaking the earth be-
neath their hoofs. Our troop of horses, urged on by our
yells, were soon in the encampment, and the savages, rushing hither and thither, trying to save themselves, were shot
and speared and cut down by swords. One desire was in
all our hearts, one cry on all lips—kill ! kill ! kill ! Such a
slaughter had not been known for a long time, and birds
and foxes and armadillos must have grown fat on the
flesh of the heathen we left for them. But we killed only
the men, and few escaped ; the women and children we
made captive.

Two days we spent in collecting the scattered cattle and
horses, numbering about ten thousand ; then with our
spoil we set out on our return and arrived at the Azul at
the end of August. On the following day the force was
broken up into the separate contingents of which it was
composed, and each in its turn was sent to the Colonel's
house to be paid. The Chascomus contingent was the
last to go up, and on presenting ourselves, each man
received two months' soldiers' pay, after which Colonel

Barboza came out and thanked us for our services, and ordered us to give up our arms at the fort and go back to our district, every man to his own house.

"We have spent some cold nights in the desert together, neighbour Nicandro," said Valerio, laughing, "but we have fared well—on raw horse flesh; and now to make it better we have received money. Why, look, with all this money I shall be able to buy a pair of new shoes for Bruno. Brave little man! I can see him toddling about among the cardoon thistles, searching for hens' eggs for his mother, and getting his poor little feet full of thorns. If there should be any change left he shall certainly have some sugar-plums."

But the others on coming to the fort began to complain loudly of the treatment they had received, when Valerio, rebuking them, told them to act like men and tell the Colonel that they were not satisfied, or else hold their peace.

"Will you, Valerio, be our spokesman?" they cried, and he consenting, they all took up their arms again and followed him back to the Colonel's house.

Barboza listened attentively to what was said and replied that our demands were just. The captives and cattle, he said, had been placed in charge of an officer appointed by the authorities and would be sold publicly in a few days. Let them now return to the fort and give up their arms, and leave Valerio with him to assist in drawing up a formal demand for their share of the spoil.

We then retired once more, giving *vivas* to our Colonel. But no sooner had we given up our arms at the fort than we were sharply ordered to saddle our horses and take our departure. I rode out with the others, but seeing that Valerio did not overtake us I went back to look for him.

This was what had happened. Left alone in his enemy's hands, Barboza had his arms taken from him, then ordered his men to carry him out to the patio and flay him alive. The men hesitated to obey so cruel a command, and this gave Valerio time to speak ; " My Colonel," he said, " you put a hard task on these poor men, and my hide when taken will be of no value to you or to them. Bid them lance me or draw a knife across my throat, and I will laud your clemency."

" You shall not lose your hide nor die," returned the Colonel, " for I admire your courage. Take him, boys, and stake him out, and give him two hundred lashes ; then throw him into the road so that it may be known that his rebellious conduct has been punished."

This order was obeyed, and out upon the road he was thrown. A compassionate store-keeper belonging to the place saw him lying there insensible, the carrion-hawks attracted by his naked bleeding body hovering about him ; and this good man took him and was ministering to him when I found him. He was lying, face down, on a pile of rugs, racked with pains, and all night long his sufferings were terrible ; nevertheless, when morning came, he insisted on setting out at once on our journey to Chascomus. When his pain was greatest and caused him to cry out, the cry, when he saw my face, would turn to a laugh. " You are too tender hearted for this world we live in," he would say. " Think nothing of this, Nicandro. I have tasted man's justice and mercy before now. Let us talk of pleasanter things. Do you know that it is the first of September to-day ? Spring has come back, though we hardly notice it yet in this cold southern country. It has been winter, winter with us, and no warmth of sun or fire, and no flowers and no birds' song. But our faces are towards the north now ; in a few days we shall sit again in the shade of the old ombú, all our toil and suffering over, to listen to the mangangá humming among the leaves and to the call of the yellow ventevéo. And better than all, little Bruno will come to us with his hands full of scarlet verbenas. Perhaps in a few years' time you, too, will be a father, Nicandro, and will know what it is to hear a child's prattle. Come, we have rested long enough, and have many leagues to ride ! "

The leagues were sixty by the road, but something was gained by leaving it, and it was easier for Valerio when the horses trod on the turf. To gallop or to trot was impossible, and even walking I had to keep at his side to support him with my arm ; for his back was all one ever-bleeding wound, and his hands were powerless, and all his joints swollen and inflamed as a result of his having been stretched out on the stakes. Five days we travelled, and day by day and night by night he grew feebler, but he would not rest ; so long as the light lasted he would be on the road ; and as we slowly pressed on, I supporting him, he would groan with pain and then laugh and begin to talk of the journey's end and of the joy of seeing wife and child again.

EL OMBÚ

It was afternoon on the fifth day when we arrived. The sight of the ombú which we had had for hours before us, strongly excited him ; he begged me, almost with tears, to urge the horses to a gallop, but it would have killed him, and I would not do it.

No person saw our approach, but the door stood open, and when we had walked our horses to within about twenty yards we heard Bruno's voice prattling to his mother. Then suddenly Valerio slipped from the saddle before I could jump down to assist him, and staggered on for a few paces towards the door. Running to his side I heard his cry—" Donata ! Bruno ! let my eyes see you ! one kiss ! " Only then his wife heard, and running out to us, saw him sink, and with one last gasp expire in my arms.

Strange and terrible scenes have I witnessed but never a sadder one than this ! Tell me, señor, are these things told in books,—does the world know them ?

Valerio was dead. He who was so brave, so generous even in his poverty, of so noble a spirit, yet so gentle ; whose words were sweeter than honey to me ! Of what his loss was to others—to that poor woman who was the mother of his one child, his little Bruno—speak not. There are things about which we must be silent, or say only, turning our eyes up, Has He forgotten us ? Does He know ? But to me the loss was greater than all losses ; for he was my friend, the man I loved above all men, who was more to me than any other, even than Santos Ugarte, whose face I should see no more.

For he, too, was dead.

And now I have once more mentioned the name of that

man, who was once so great in this district, let me, there-fore proceeding with the history of El Ombú, tell you his end. I heard of it by chance long after he had been placed under the ground.

It was the old man's custom in that house, on the other side of the Rio de la Plata where he was obliged to live, to go down every day to the water-side. Long hours would be spent there, sitting on the rocks, always with his face towards Buenos Ayres. He was waiting, waiting for the pardon which would, perhaps, in God's good time, come to him from that forgetful place. He was thinking of El Ombú ; for what was life to him away from it, in that strange country ? And that unsatisfied desire, and perhaps remorse, had, they say, made his face terrible to look at, for it was like the face of a dead man who had died with wide-open eyes.

One day some boatmen on the beach noticed that he was seated on the rocks far out and that when the tide rose he made no movement to escape from the water. They saw him sitting waist-deep in the sea, and when they rescued him from his perilous position and brought him to the shore, he stared at them like a great white owl and talked in a strange way.

" It is very cold and very dark," he said, " and I cannot see your faces, but perhaps you know me. I am Santos Ugarte, of El Ombú. I have had a great misfortune, friends. To-day in my anger I killed a poor youth whom I loved like a son—my poor boy Meliton ! Why did he despise my warning and put himself in my way ! But I will say no more about that. After killing him I rode away with the intention of going to Buenos Ayres, but on the road I repented of my deed and turned back. I said that with my own hands I would take him up and carry him in, and call my neighbours together to watch with me by his poor body. But, Sirs, the night overtook me and the Sanborombón is swollen with rains, as you no doubt know, and in swimming it I lost my horse. I do not know if he was drowned. Let me have a fresh horse, friends, and show me the way to El Ombú, and God will reward you."

In that delusion he remained till the end, a few days later, when he died. May his soul rest in peace !

CHAPTER V

SEÑOR, when I am here and remember these things, I
sometimes say to myself: Why, old man, do you
come to this tree to sit for an hour in the shade, since there
is not on all these plains a sadder or more bitter place?
My answer is: To one who has lived long, there is no house
and no spot of ground, overgrown with grass and weeds,
where a house once stood and where men have lived, that
is not equally sad. For this sadness is in us, in a memory
of other days which follows us into all places. But for the
child there is no past: he is born into the world light
hearted like a bird; for him gladness is everywhere.

That is how it was with little Bruno, too young to feel
the loss of a father or to remember him long. It was her
great love of this child which enabled Donata to live
through so terrible a calamity. She never quitted El
Ombú. An embargo had been placed on the estancia so
that it could not be sold, and she was not disturbed in her
possession of the house. She now shared it with an old
married couple, who, being poor and having a few animals,
were glad of a place to live in rent free. The man, whose
name was Pascual, took care of Donata's flock and the few
cows and horses she owned along with his own. He was a
simple, good-tempered old man, whose only fault was
indolence, and a love of the bottle and of play. But that

mattered little, for when he gambled he invariably lost, through not being sober, so that when he had any money it was quickly gone.

Old Pascual first put Bruno on a horse and taught him to ride after the flock, and to do a hundred things. The boy was like his father, of a beautiful countenance, with black curling hair, and eyes as lively as a bird's. It was not strange that Donata loved him as no mother ever loved a son, but as he grew up a perpetual anxiety was in her heart lest he should hear the story of his father's death and the cause of it. For she was wise in this ; she knew that the most dangerous of all passions is that of revenge, since when it enters into the heart all others, good or bad, are driven out, and all ties and interests and all the words that can be uttered are powerless to restrain a man ; and the end is ruin. Many times she spoke of this to me, begging me with tears never to speak of my dead friend to Bruno, lest he should discover the truth, and that fatal rage should enter into his heart.

It had been Donata's custom, every day since Valerio's death, to take a pitcher of water, fresh from the well, and pour it out on the ground, on the spot where he had sunk down and expired, without that sight of wife and child, that one kiss, for which he had cried. Who can say what caused her to do such a thing? A great grief is like a delirium, and sometimes gives us strange thoughts, and makes us act like demented persons. It may have been because of the appearance of the dead face as she first saw it, dry and white as ashes, the baked black lips, the look of thirst that would give everything for a drink of cold water; and that which she had done in the days of anguish, of delirium, she had continued to do.

The spot where the water was poured each day being but a few yards from the door of the house was of a dryness and hardness of fire-baked bricks, trodden hard by the feet of I know not how many generations of men, and by hoofs of horses ridden every day to the door. But after a long time of watering a little green began to appear in the one spot; and the green was of a creeping plant with small round malva-like leaves, and little white flowers like porcelain shirt buttons. It spread and thickened, and was like a soft green carpet about two yards long placed on that dry ground, and it was of an emerald greenness all the year round, even in the hot weather when the grass was dead and dry and the plains were in colour like a faded yellow rag.

When Bruno was a boy of fourteen I went one day to help him in making a sheepfold, and when our work was finished in the afternoon we went to the house to sip maté. Before going in, on coming to that green patch, Bruno cried out, " Have you ever seen so verdant a spot as this, Nicandro, so soft and cool a spot to lie down on when one is hot and tired ? " He then threw himself down full length upon it, and, lying at ease on his back, he looked up at Donata, who had come out to us, and spoke laughingly, " Ah, little mother of my soul ! A thousand times have I asked you why you poured water every day on this spot and you would not tell me. Now I have found out. It was all to make me a soft cool spot to lie on when I come back tired and hot from work. Look ! is it not like a soft bed with a green and white velvet coverlid ; bring water now, mother mine, and pour it on my hot, dusty face."

She laughed, too, poor woman, but I could see the tears in her eyes—the tears which she was always so careful to hide from him.

All this I remember as if it had happened yesterday ; I can see and hear it all—Donata's laugh and the tears in her eyes which Bruno could not see. I remember it so well because this was almost the last time I saw her before I was compelled to go away, for my absence was long. But before I speak of that change let me tell you of something that happened about two years before at El Ombú, which brought a new happiness into that poor widow's life.

It happened that among those that had no right to be on the land, but came and settled there because there was no one to forbid them, there was a man named Sanchez, who had built himself a small rancho about half a league from the old house, and kept a flock of sheep. He was a widower with one child, a little girl named Monica. This Sanchez, although poor, was not a good man, and had no tenderness in his heart. He was a gambler, always away from his rancho, leaving the flock to be taken care of by poor little Monica. In winter it was cruel, for then the sheep travel most, and most of all on cold, rough days ; and she without a dog to help her, barefooted on the thistle-grown land, often in terror at the sight of cattle, would be compelled to spend the whole day out of doors. More than once on a winter evening in bad weather I have found her trying to drive the sheep home in the face of the rain, crying with misery. It hurt me all the more because she had a pretty face : no person could fail to see its beauty, though she was in rags and her black hair in a tangle, like the mane of a horse that has been feeding among the burrs. At such times I have taken her up on my saddle and driven her flock home for her, and have said to myself : " Poor lamb without a mother, if you were mine I would seat you on the horns of the moon ; but, unhappy one ! he whom you call father is without compassion."

At length, Sanchez, finding himself without money, just when strangers from all places were coming to Chascomus to witness a great race and anxious not to lose this chance of large winnings, sold his sheep, having nothing of more value to dispose of. But instead of winning he lost, and then leaving Monica in a neighbour's house he went away, promising to return for her in a few days. But he did not return, and it was believed by everybody that he had abandoned the child.

It was then that Donata offered to take her and be a mother to the orphan, and I can say, señor, that the poor child's own mother, who was dead, could not have treated her more tenderly or loved her more. And the pretty one had now been Donata's little daughter and Bruno's playmate two years when I was called away, and I saw them not again and heard no tidings of them for a space of five years—the five longest years of my life.

CHAPTER VI

I WENT away because men were wanted for the army, and I was taken. I was away, I have said, five years, and the five would have been ten, and the ten twenty, supposing that life had lasted, but for a lance wound in my thigh, which made me a lame man for the rest of my life. That was the reason of my discharge and happy escape from that purgatory. Once back in these plains where I first saw heaven's light, I said in my heart : I can no longer spring light as a bird on to the back of an unbroken animal and laugh at his efforts to shake me off ; nor can I throw a lasso on a running horse or bull and digging my heel in the ground, pit my strength against his ; nor can I ever be what I have been in any work or game on horseback or on foot ; nevertheless, this lameness, and all I have lost through it, is a small price to pay for my deliverance.

But this is not the history of my life ; let me remember that I speak only of those who have lived at El Ombú in my time, in the old house which no longer exists.

There had been no changes when I returned, except that those five years had made Bruno almost a man, and more than ever like his father, except that he never had that I-know-not-what something to love in the eyes which made Valerio different from all men. Donata was

37

the same, but older. Grey hair had come to her in her affliction ; now her hair which should have been black was all white—but she was more at peace, for Bruno was good to her, and as a widow's only son, was exempt from military service. There was something else to make her happy. Those two, who were everything to her, could not grow up under one roof and not love ; now she could look with confidence to a union between them, and there would be no separation. But even so, that old fear she had so often spoken of to me in former days was never absent from her heart.

Bruno was now away most of the time, working as a cattle drover, his ambition being, Donata informed me, to make money so as to buy everything needed for the house.

I had been back, living in that poor rancho, half a league from El Ombú, where I first saw the light, for the best part of a year, when Bruno, who had been away with his employer buying cattle in the south, one day appeared at my place. He had not been to El Ombú, and was silent and strange in his manner, and when we were alone together I said to him : " What has happened to you, Bruno, that you have the face of a stranger and speak in an unaccustomed tone to your friend ? "

He answered : " Because you, Nicandro, have treated me like a child, concealing from me that which you ought to have told me long ago, instead of leaving me to learn it by accident from a stranger."

" It has come," I said to myself, for I knew what he meant : then I spoke of his mother.

38

"Ah, yes," he said with bitterness, "I know now why she pours water fresh from the well every day on the spot of ground near the door. Do you, Nicandro, think that water will ever wash away that old stain and memory? A man who is a man, must in such a thing obey, not a mother's wish, nor any woman, but that something which speaks in his heart."

"Let no such thought dwell in you to make you mad," I replied. "Look, Bruno, my friend's son and my friend, leave it to God who is above us, and who considers and remembers all evil deeds that men do, and desires not that anyone should take the sword out of His hand."

"Who is He—this God you talk of?" he answered. "Have you seen or spoken with Him that you tell me what His mind is in this matter? I have only this voice to tell me how a man should act in such a case," and he smote his breast; then overcome with a passion of grief he covered his face with his hands and wept.

Vainly I begged him not to lose himself, telling him what the effect of his attempt, whether he succeeded or failed, would be on Donata and on Monica—it would break those poor women's hearts. I spoke, too, of things I had witnessed in my five years' service; the cruel sentences from which there was no appeal, the torments, the horrible deaths so often inflicted. For these evils there was no remedy on earth : and he, a poor, ignorant boy, what would he do but dash himself to pieces against that tower of brass !

He replied that within that brazen tower there was a heart full of blood ; and with that he went away, only asking me as a favour not to tell his mother of this visit to me.

Some ten days later she had a message from him, brought from the capitol by a traveller going to the south. Bruno sent word that he was going to Las Mulitas, a place fifty leagues west of Buenos Ayres, to work on an estancia there, and would be absent some months.

Why had he gone thither? Because he had heard that General Barboza—for that man was now a General— owned a tract of land at that place, which the Government had given him as a reward for his services on the southern frontier; and that he had recently returned from the northern provinces to Buenos Ayres and was now staying at this estancia at Las Mulitas.

Donata knew nothing of his secret motives, but his absence filled her with anxiety; and when at length she fell ill I resolved to go in search of the poor youth and try to persuade him to return to El Ombú. But at Las Mulitas I heard that he was no longer there. All strangers had been taken for the army in the frontier department, and Bruno, in spite of his passport, had been forced to go.

When I returned to El Ombú with this sad news Donata resolved at once to go to the capitol and try to obtain his release. She was ill, and it was a long journey for her to perform on horseback, but she had friends to go with and take care of her. In the end she succeeded in seeing the President, and throwing herself on her knees before him, and with tears in her eyes, implored him to let her have her son back.

He listened to her, and gave her a paper to take to the

War Office. There it was found that Bruno had been sent to El Rosario, and an order was despatched for his immediate release. But when the order reached its destination the unhappy boy had deserted.

That was the last that Donata ever heard of her son. She guessed why he had gone, and knew, as well as if I had told her, that he had found out the secret so long hidden from him. Still, being his mother, she would not abandon hope; she struggled to live. Never did I come into her presence but I saw in her face a question which she dared not put in words. If, it said, you have heard, if you know, when and how his life ended, tell me now before I go. But it also said : If you know, do not tell me so that I and Monica may go on hoping together to the end.

" I know, Nicandro," she would say, " that if Bruno returns he will not be the same—the son I have lost. For in that one thing he is not like his father. Could another be like Valerio ? No misfortune and no injustice could change that heart, or turn his sweetness sour. In that freshness and gaiety of temper he was like a child, and Bruno as a child was like him. My son ! my son ! where are you ? God of my soul, grant that he may yet come to me, though his life be now darkened with some terrible passion—though his poor hands be stained with blood, so that my eyes may see him again before I go ! "

But he came not, and she died without seeing him.

CHAPTER VII

IF Monica, left alone in the house with old Pascual and his wife, had been disposed to listen to those who were attracted by her face she might have found a protector worthy of her. There were men of substance among those who came for her. But it mattered nothing to her whether they had land and cattle or not, or what their appearance was, and how they were dressed. Hers was a faithful heart. And she looked for Bruno's return, not with that poor half-despairing hope which had been Donata's and had failed to keep her alive, but with a hope that sustained and made her able to support the months and years of waiting. She looked for his coming as the night-watcher for the dawn. On summer afternoons, when the heat of the day was over, she would take her sewing outside the gate and sit there by the hour, where her sight commanded the road to the north. From that side he would certainly come. On dark, rainy nights a lantern would be hung on the wall lest he, coming at a late hour, should miss the house in the dark. Glad she was not, nor lively; she was pale and thin, and those dark eyes that looked too large because of her thinness were the eyes of one who had beheld grief. But with it all, there was a serenity, an air of one whose tears, held back, would all be shed at the proper time, when he returned. And he would, perhaps, come to-day, or, if not to-day, then to-morrow, or perhaps the day after, as God willed.

Nearly three years had passed by since Donata's death when, one afternoon, I rode to El Ombú, and on approaching the house spied a saddled horse, which had got loose, going away at a trot. I went after, and caught, and led it back, and then saw that its owner was a traveller, an old soldier, who with or without the permission of the people of the house, was lying down and asleep in the shade of the ombú.

There had lately been a battle in the northern part of the province, and the defeated force had broken up, and the men carrying their arms had scattered themselves all over the country. This veteran was one of them.

He did not wake when I led the horse up and shouted to him. He was a man about fifty to sixty years old, grey-haired, with many scars of sword and lance wounds on his sun-blackened face and hands. His carbine was leaning against the tree a yard or two away, but he had not unbuckled his sword, and what now attracted my attention as I sat on my horse regarding him, was the way in which he clutched the hilt and shook the weapon until it rattled in its scabbard. His was an agitated sleep ; the sweat stood in big drops on his face, he ground his teeth and moaned, and muttered words which I could not catch.

At length, dismounting, I called to him again, then shouted in his ear, and finally shook him by the shoulder. Then he woke with a start, and struggling up to a sitting position, and staring at me like one demented, he exclaimed, " What has happened ? "

When I told him about his horse he was silent, and, sitting there with eyes cast down, passed his hand repeatedly across his forehead. Never in any man's face had I seen misery compared to his. " Pardon me, friend," he spoke at last. " My ears were so full of sounds you do not hear that I paid little attention to what you were saying."

" Perhaps the great heat of the day has overcome you," I said. " Or maybe you are suffering from some malady caused by an old wound received in fight."

" Yes, an incurable malady," he returned, gloomily. " Have you, friend, been in the army ? "

" Five years had I served when a wound which made me lame for life delivered me from that hell."

" I have served thirty," he returned, " perhaps more. I know that I was very young when I was taken and I remember that a woman I called mother wept to see me go. That any eyes should have shed tears for me ! Shall I now in that place in the South where I was born find one who remembers my name ? I look not for it ! I have no one but this "—and here he touched his sword.

After an interval, he continued, " We say, friend, that in the army we can do no wrong, since all responsibility rests with those who are over us ; that our most cruel and sanguinary deeds are no more a sin or crime than is the shedding of the blood of cattle, or of Indians who are not Christians, and are therefore of no more account than cattle in God's sight. We say, too, that once we have

44

become accustomed to kill, not men only, but even those who are powerless to defend themselves—the weak and the innocent—we think nothing of it, and have no compunction nor remorse. If this be so, why does He, the One who is above, torment me before my time? Is it just? Listen: no sooner do I close my eyes than sleep brings to me that most terrible experience a man can have—to be in the midst of a conflict and powerless. The bugles call: there is a movement everywhere of masses of men, foot and horse, and every face has on it the look of one who is doomed. There is a murmur of talking all round me, the officers are shouting and waving their swords; I strive in vain to catch the word of command; I do not know what is happening; it is all confusion, a gloom of smoke and dust, a roar of guns, a great noise and shouting of the enemy charging through us. And I am helpless. I wake, and slowly the noise and terrible scene fade from my mind, only to return when sleep again overcomes me. What repose, what refreshment can I know! Sleep, they say, is a friend to everyone, and makes all equal, the rich and the poor, the guilty and the innocent; they say, too, that this forgetfulness is like a draught of cold water to the thirsty man. But what shall I say of sleep? Often with this blade would I have delivered myself from its torture but for the fear that there may be after death something even worse than this dream."

After an interval of silence, seeing that he had recovered from his agitation, I invited him to go with me to the house. " I see smoke issuing from the kitchen," I said,

" let us go in so that you may refresh yourself with maté before resuming your journey."

We went in and found the old people boiling the kettle ; and in a little while Monica came in and sat with us. Never did she greet one without that light which was like sunshine in her dark eyes ; words were not needed to tell me of the gratitude and friendliness she felt toward me, for she was not one to forget the past. I remember that she looked well that day in her white dress with a red flower. Had not Bruno said that he liked to see her in white, and that a flower on her bosom or in her hair was an ornament that gave her most grace ? And Bruno might arrive at any moment. But the sight of that grey-haired veteran in his soiled and frayed uniform, and with his clanking sword and his dark scarred face, greatly disturbed her. I noticed that she grew paler and could scarcely keep her eyes off his face while he talked.

While sipping his maté he told us of fights he had been in, of long marches and sufferings in desert places, and of some of the former men he had served under. Among them he, by chance, named General Barboza.

Monica, I knew, had never heard of that man, and on this account I feared not to speak of him. It had, I said, been reported, I knew not whether truthfully or not, that Barboza was dead.

" On that point I can satisfy you," he returned, " since I was serving with him, when his life came to an end in the province of San Luis about two years ago. He was at the head of nineteen hundred men when it happened, and the whole force was filled with amazement at the event. Not that they regretted his loss ; on the contrary, his own followers feared, and were glad to be delivered from him. He exceeded most commanders in ferocity, and was accustomed to say scoffingly to his prisoners that he would not have gunpowder wasted on them. ` That was not a thing to complain of, but he was capable of treating his own men as he treated a spy or a prisoner of war. Many a one have I seen put to death with a blunted knife, he, Barboza, looking on, smoking a cigarette. It was the manner of his death that startled us, for never had man been seen to perish in such a way.

" It happened on this march, about a month before the end, that a soldier named Bracamonte went one day at noon to deliver a letter from his captain to the General. Barboza was sitting in his shirt-sleeves in his tent when the letter was handed to him, but just when he put out his hand to take it the man made an attempt to stab him. The General throwing himself back escaped the blow, then instantly sprang like a tiger upon his assailant, and seizing him by the wrist, wrenched the weapon out of his hand only to strike it quick as lightning into the poor fool's throat. No sooner was he down than the General bending over him, before drawing out the weapon, called to those who had run to his assistance to get him a tumbler. When, tumbler in hand, he lifted himself up and looked upon them, they say that his face was of the whiteness of iron made white in the furnace, and that his eyes were like two flames. He was mad with rage, and cried out with a loud voice, " Thus, in the presence of the army, do I serve the wretch who thought to shed my blood ! "

Then with a furious gesture he threw down and shattered the reddened glass, and bade them take the dead man outside the camp and leave him stripped to the vultures.

" This ended the episode, but from that day it was noticed by those about him that a change had come over the General. If, friend, you have served with, or have even seen him, you know the man he was—tall and well-formed, blue eyes and fair like an Englishman, endowed with a strength, endurance and resolution that was a wonder to everyone : he was like an eagle among birds— that great bird that has no weakness and no mercy, whose cry fills all creatures with dismay, whose pleasure it is to tear his victim's flesh with his crooked talons. But now some secret malady had fallen on him which took away all his mighty strength ; the colour of his face changed to sickly paleness, and he bent forward and swayed this way and that in the saddle as he rode like a drunken man, and this strange weakness increased day by day. It was said in the army that the blood of the man he had killed had poisoned him. The doctors who accompanied us in this march could not cure him, and their failure so angered him against them that they began to fear for their own safety. They now said that he could not be properly treated in camp, but must withdraw to some town where a different system could be followed ; but this he refused to do.

" Now it happened that we had an old soldier with us who was a curandero. He was a native of Santa Fé, and was famed for his cures in his own department ; but having had the misfortune to kill a man, he was arrested and condemned to serve ten years in the army. This person now informed some of the officers that he would under-take to cure the General, and Barboza, hearing of it, sent for and questioned him. The curandero informed him that his malady was one which the doctors could not cure. It was a failure of a natural heat of the blood, and only by means of animal heat, not by drugs, could health be recovered. In such a grave case the usual remedy of putting the feet and legs in the body of some living animal opened for the purpose would not be sufficient. Some very large beast should be procured and the patient placed bodily in it.

" The General agreed to submit himself to this treat-ment ; the doctors dared not interfere, and men were sent out in quest of a large animal. We were then encamped on a wide sandy plain in San Luis, and as we were without tents we were suffering much from the great heat and the dust-laden winds. But at this spot the General had grown worse, so that he could no longer sit on his horse, and here we had to wait for his improvement.

" In due time a very big bull was brought in and fastened to a stake in the middle of the camp. A space, fifty or sixty yards round, was marked out and roped round, and ponchos hung on the rope to form a curtain so that what was being done should not be witnessed by the army. But a great curiosity and anxiety took pos-session of the entire force, and when the bull was thrown down and his agonising bellowings were heard, from all sides officers and men began to move toward that fatal spot. It had been noised about that the cure would be almost instantaneous, and many were prepared to greet the reappearance of the General with a loud cheer.

" Then very suddenly, almost before the bellowings had ceased, shrieks were heard from the enclosure, and in a moment, while we all stood staring and wondering, out rushed the General, stark naked, reddened with that bath of warm blood he had been in, a sword which he had hastily snatched up in his hand. Leaping over the barrier, he stood still for an instant, then catching sight of the great mass of men before him he flew at them, yelling and whirling his sword round so that it looked like a shining wheel in the sun. The men seeing that he was raving mad fled before him, and for a space of a hundred yards or more he pursued them ; then the superhuman energy was ended ; the sword flew from his hand, he staggered, and fell prostrate on the earth. For some minutes no one ventured to approach him, but he never stirred, and at length, when examined, was found to be dead."

The soldier had finished his story, and though I had many questions to ask I asked none, for I saw Monica's distress, and that she had gone white even to the lips at the terrible things the man had related. But now he had ended, and would soon depart, for the sun was getting low.

He rolled up and lighted a cigarette, and was about to rise from the bench, when he said, " One thing I forgot to mention about the soldier Bracamonte, who attempted to assassinate the General. After he had been carried out and stripped for the vultures, a paper was found sewn up in the lining of his tunic, which proved to be his passport, for it contained his right description. It said that he was a native of this department of Chascomus, so that you may have heard of him. His name was Bruno de la Cueva."

Would that he had not spoken those last words! Never, though I live to be a hundred, shall I forget that terrible scream that came from Monica's lips before she fell senseless to the floor!

As I raised her in my arms, the soldier turned and said, " She is subject to fits ? "

" No," I replied, " that Bruno, of whose death we have now heard for the first time, was of this house."

" It was destiny that led me to this place," he said, " or perhaps that God who is ever against me ; but you, friend, are my witness that I crossed not this threshold with a drawn weapon in my hand." And with these words he took his departure, and from that day to this I have never again beheld his face.

She opened her eyes at last, but the wings of my heart drooped when I saw them, since it was easy to see that she had lost her reason ; but whether that calamity or the grief she would have known is greatest who can say ? Some have died of pure grief—did it not kill Donata in the end ?—but the crazed may live many years. We sometimes think it would be better if they were dead ; but not in all cases—not, señor, in this.

She lived on here with the old people, for from the first she was quiet and docile as a child. Finally an order came from a person in authority at Chascomus for those who were in the house to quit it. It was going to be pulled down for the sake of the material which was required for a building in the village. Pascual died about that time, and the widow, now old and infirm, went to live with some poor relations at Chascomus and took Monica with her. When the old woman died Monica remained with these people : she lives with them to this day. But she is free to come and go at will, and is known to all in the village as *la loca del Ombú*. They are kind to her, for her story is known to them, and God has put compassion in their hearts.

To see her you would hardly believe that she is the Monica I have told you of, whom I knew as a little one, running bare-footed after her father's flock. For she has grey hairs and wrinkles now. As you ride to Chascomus from this point you will see, on approaching the lake, a very high bank on your left hand, covered with a growth of tall fennel, hoarhound, and cardoon thistle. There on most days you will find her, sitting on the bank in the shade of the tall fennel bushes, looking across the water. She watches for the flamingos. There are many of those great birds on the lake, and they go in flocks, and when they rise and travel across the water, flying low, their scarlet wings may be seen at a great distance. And every time she catches sight of a flock moving like a red line across the lake she cries out with delight. That is her one happiness—her life. And she is the last of all those who have lived in my time at El Ombú.

APPENDIX TO EL OMBÚ

APPENDIX TO EL OMBÚ

The English Invasion and the Game of El Pato

I MUST say at once that El Ombú is mostly a true story, although the events did not occur exactly in the order given. The incident relating to the English invasion of June and July, 1807, is told pretty much as I had it from the old gaucho called Nicandro in the narrative. That was in the 'sixties. The undated notes which I made of my talks with the old man, containing numerous anecdotes of Santos Ugarte and the whole history of El Ombú, were written, I think, in 1868—the year of the great dust storm. These ancient notes are now before me, and look very strange, both as to the writing and the quality of the paper; also as to the dirtiness of the same, which makes me think that the old manuscript must have been out in that memorable storm, which, I remember, ended with rain—the rain coming down as liquid mud.

There were other old men living in that part of the country who, as boys, had witnessed the march of an English army on Buenos Ayres, and one of these confirmed the story of the blankets thrown away by the army, and of the chaff between some of the British soldiers and the natives.

I confess I had some doubts as to the truth of this

blanket story when I came to read over my old notes ; but in referring to the proceedings of the court-martial on Lieutenant-General Whitelocke, published in London in 1808, I find that the incident is referred to. On page 57 of the first volume occurs the following statement, made by General Gower in his evidence. " The men, particularly of Brigadier-General Lumley's brigade, were very much exhausted, and Lieutenant-General White-locke, to give them a chance of getting on with tolerable rapidity, ordered all the blankets of the army to be thrown down."

There is nothing, however, in the evidence about the blankets having been used to make a firmer bottom for the army to cross a river, nor is the name of the river mentioned.

Another point in the old gaucho's story may strike the English reader as very strange and almost incredible ; this is, that within a very few miles of the army of the hated foreign invader, during its march on the capital, where the greatest excitement prevailed and every pre-paration for defence was being made, a large number of men were amusing themselves at the game of El Pato. To those who are acquainted with the character of the gaucho there is nothing incredible in such a fact ; for the gaucho is, or was, absolutely devoid of the sentiment of patriotism, and regarded all rulers, all in authority from the highest to the lowest, as his chief enemies, and the worst kind of robbers, since they robbed him not only of his goods but of his liberty.

It mattered not to him whether his country paid tribute

to Spain or to England, whether a man appointed by someone at a distance as Governor or Viceroy had black or blue eyes. It was seen that when the Spanish dominion came to an end his hatred was transferred to the ruling cliques of a so-called Republic. When the gauchos attached themselves to Rosas, and assisted him to climb into power, they were under the delusion that he was one of themselves, and would give them that perfect liberty to live their own lives in their own way, which is their only desire. They found out their mistake when it was too late.

It was Rosas who abolished the game of El Pato, but before saying more on that point it would be best to describe the game. I have never seen an account of it in print, but for a very long period, and down to probably about 1840, it was the most popular outdoor game on the Argentine pampas. Doubtless it originated there; it was certainly admirably suited to the habits and disposition of the horsemen of the plains; and unlike most outdoor games it retained its original simple, rude character to the end.

Pato means duck; and to play the game a duck or fowl, or, as was usually the case, some larger domestic bird —turkey, gosling, or muscovy duck—was killed and sewn up in a piece of stout raw hide, forming a somewhat shapeless ball, twice as big as a football, and provided with four loops or handles of strong twisted raw hide made of a convenient size to be grasped by a man's hand. A great point was to have the ball and handles so strongly made that three or four powerful men could take hold and tug until they dragged each other to the ground without anything giving way.

Whenever it was resolved at any place to have a game, and someone had offered to provide the bird, and the meeting place had been settled, notice would be sent round among the neighbours ; and at the appointed time all the men and youths living within a circle of several leagues would appear on the spot, mounted on their best horses. On the appearance of the man on the ground carrying the duck the others would give chase ; and by-and-by he would be overtaken, and the ball wrested from his hand ; the victor in his turn would be pursued, and when overtaken there would perhaps be a scuffle or scrimmage, as in football, only the strugglers would be first on horseback before dragging each other to the earth. Occasionally when this happened a couple of hot-headed players, angry at being hurt or worsted, would draw their weapons against each other in order to find who was in the right, or to prove which was the better man. But fight or no fight, someone would get the duck and carry it away to be chased again. Leagues of ground would be gone over by the players in this way, and at last some one, luckier or better mounted than his fellows, would get the duck and successfully run the gauntlet of the people scattered about on the plain, and make good his escape. He was the victor, and it was his right to carry the bird home and have it for his dinner. This was, however, a mere fiction ; the man who carried off the duck made for the nearest house, followed by all the others, and there not only the duck was cooked, but a vast amount of meat to feed the

whole of the players. While the dinner was in prepara-
tion, messengers would be despatched to neighbouring
houses to invite the women ; and on their arrival dancing
would be started and kept up all night.

To the gauchos of the great plains, who took to the back
of a horse from childhood, almost as spontaneously as a
parasite to the animal on which it feeds, the pato was the
game of games, and in their country as much as cricket
and football and golf together to the inhabitants of this
island. Nor could there have been any better game for
men whose existence, or whose success in life, depended
so much on their horsemanship ; and whose chief glory it
was to be able to stick on under difficulties, and, when
sticking on was impossible, to fall off gracefully and like a
cat, on their feet. To this game the people of the pampa
were devoted up to a time when it came into the head of
a President of the Republic to have no more of it, and
with a stroke of the pen it was abolished for ever.

It would take a strong man in this country to put down
any outdoor game to which the people are attached ; and
he was assuredly a very strong man who did away with
El Pato in that land. If any other man who has occupied
the position of head of the State at any time during the
last ninety years had attempted such a thing, a universal
shout of derision would have been the result, and wherever
such an absurd decree had appeared pasted up on the
walls and doors of churches, shops, and other public
places, the gauchos would have been seen filling their
mouths with water to squirt it over the despised paper.
But this man was more than a president ; he was that

59

APPENDIX TO EL OMBÚ

Rosas, called by his enemies the "Nero of America." Though by birth a member of a distinguished family, he was by predilection a gaucho, and early in life took to the semi-barbarous life of the plains. Among his fellows Rosas distinguished himself as a dare-devil, one who was not afraid to throw himself from the back of his own horse on to that of a wild horse in the midst of a flying herd into which he had charged. He had all the gaucho's native ferocity, his fierce hates and prejudices; and it was in fact his intimate knowledge of the people he lived with, his oneness in mind with them, that gave him his wonderful influence over them, and enabled him to carry out his ambitious schemes. But why, when he had succeeded in making himself all-powerful by means of their help, when he owed them so much, and the ties uniting him to them were so close, did he deprive them of their beloved pastime? The reason, which will sound almost ridiculous after what I have said of the man's character, was that he considered the game too rough. It is true that it had (for him) its advantages, since it made the men of the plains hardy, daring, resourceful fighters on horseback— the kind of men he most needed for his wars; on the other hand, it caused so much injury to the players, and resulted in so many bloody fights and fierce feuds between neighbours that he considered he lost more than he gained by it.

There were not men enough in the country for his wants; even boys of twelve and fourteen were sometimes torn from the arms of their weeping mothers to be made soldiers of; he could not afford to have full-grown strong men injuring and killing each other for their own amusement. They must, like good citizens, sacrifice their pleasure for their country's sake. And at length, when his twenty years' reign was over, when people were again free to follow their own inclinations without fear of bullet and cold steel—it was generally cold steel in those days—those who had previously played the game had had roughness enough in their lives, and now only wanted rest and ease ; while the young men and youths who had not taken part in El Pato nor seen it played, had never come under its fascination, and had no wish to see it revived.